SKEETER'S ISLAND ADVENTURE

By Christopher Nance

Christopher Nance
NBC-70

Illustrated By
Michael Rich & Mark Bennett

First Edition

Text copyright © 1999 by Christopher Nance
Christopher Productions Inc.
CPI Publishers © copyright 1999

Printed in Singapore by Eurasia Press Pte Ltd

Published by Christopher Productions Inc.
CPI Publishers
10153 1/2 Riverside Drive, #266
Toluca Lake, CA 91602
(888) 831-9268

Nicholette Ortega Nance, Publisher
Tanya Light, Editor

ISBN 0-9648363-5-1
Library of Congress Catalog Card Number 98-094836

Acknowledgments

Special thanks to Tanya Light for the editing of this book.

Special thanks to Paul Villar, my personal assistant, for all the hard work and long hours.

Special thanks to Bonnie Selman for all the hard work and long hours.

Special thanks to my darling Sam. My editor, publisher and best friend.

Words From The Author

I offer this book to all that share my love for God. I was born with a life-threatening illness that was supposed to end my life when I was a child. My Lord had and still has (I hope) plans for my future. Whether I am on television, doing speaking engagements or writing books, I owe all the glory to God.

The character in this story is very much like myself. Skeeter helps people who are in need. He loves nature and life around him and he looks for the good in everyone. I believe the key to being happy with our life on earth is to stay true to your relationship with God. Develop the skills that the good Lord gave you and then use those skills to make this world a better place.

Christopher Nance
Author

It was a perfect day and Skeeter was flying high.
Only a few, tiny clouds decorated the sky.

Then came a sobbing sound from out over the sea.
Skeeter flew all around to see what it could be.

Look, two baby clouds are making that fuss.
"Our mother and father have gone without us."

Mom and Dad were caught in a big storm and
the winds blew so strong,
that these baby clouds just could not tag along.

"Don't worry," smiled Skeeter.
"I know what to do!
I'll catch up with your folks and bring
them back to you."

With a blink of an eye Skeeter zoomed
straight up top,
going higher and higher to look for their
Mom and Pop.

He zoomed to the left and then he zoomed
to the right,
but as far as the eye could see, there were no
clouds in sight.

Skeeter didn't want to face the two baby clouds,
so he flew back dejected, with his head
sadly bowed.

"Did you find them?" the babies asked. "Did you see our Mom and Dad?"

Skeeter did not answer.
He was just too sad.

"Your parents will come back. Trust in God. Just you wait and see.
Don't give up hope. Just leave it to me."

So the big, red airplane rolled over and flew down low,
past sea gulls and cargo ships and things that moved slow.

He wanted to desperately help them in his attempts, he would not fail.

Skeeter flew toward an island, following a pod of gray whales.

As he swooped across the island heading
straight for the ground,
he noticed all the grass was ugly and brown.

"What happened to all the grass?" asked Skeeter to a herd of buffalo.
"We've had no rain," cried the leader, "no rain to make the grass grow."

The baby calves were all thirsty and started to cry.
Without rain Skeeter feared that the wildlife would die.

The fish in the lake could sure use
a good flood,
where the boy and his grandpa were
fishing in mud.

All the trees and plants were dying.
There was no water to be found.
If someone didn't do something, the whole island
would soon turn brown.

Just then Skeeter came up with a wonderful idea.
By using his propeller, he would blow the clouds
over here.

"I shall be back," yelled Skeeter to the buffalo
and the fish.
"Hang on and keep living," was the excited
plane's wish.

As fast as he could, Skeeter flew across the sky
toward the two baby clouds that were
still nearby.

"Your parents won't be coming back quite
so soon
but I've found a nice place where you will
have lots of room."

"That little island needs water and some cool shade.
You would both be welcome, if you wanted to stay."

"But how will we get there? It looks terribly far. We are moved by the wind, and there has been none so far."

Skeeter smiled. "Just leave that to me. I know what to do.
I will rev up my engine and fly backwards toward you."

Skeeter's engine roared loudly and the wind started to blow.
Then inch by inch, very slowly, both clouds started to go.

Skeeter directed the wind with his wings
and his tail,
and the two clouds were moving
just like a big sail!

"Weeeeeeeeee, you are doing it. The island is getting near!"
But Skeeter was making such a racket, he just could not hear.

He pushed and he blew like a big ceiling fan,

until the clouds drifted over the thirsty land.

Skeeter was tired. Indeed, he was all worn out.
His engine was sputtering as he said
with a shout,
"I've done my best. It's all up to you."
The clouds replied,
"Just leave it to us, Skeeter. We know
what to do!"

And with that the clouds rumbled. The air started to blow.
Drops of rainwater fell down on the dry buffalo.

The lakes started to fill with raindrops. Skeeter now had to continue the search for Mom and Pop.

But off in the distance came
flashes of bright light,
then a loud booming sound
that gave Skeeter a fright.

"Get away from our babies! Leave them alone!"
The baby clouds replied, "Mommy, Daddy,
you've finally come home."
The baby clouds then explained that Skeeter
was a friend, and how in their absence,
he looked after them.

The grown up clouds nodded and
gave Skeeter a fluffy hug.
Skeeter blushed bright red
and said with a shrug,
"Everyone needs someone.
It's no fun being alone.
I'm so glad that this family can
call this place home."

So the next time you see an island so beautiful
and green,
just think of Skeeter and remember
this scene.

We all can be heroes, just give it a try.
Believe in yourself and then reach for the sky.

Dream lofty dreams and make them come true.
With God in your heart, there is nothing you
can't do.

The End

HOW MANY OF MY BOOKS HAVE YOU READ ?
- *MUHAMMAD AND THE MARATHON*
- *BEFORE THERE WERE PEOPLE*
- *THE WEATHERMAN IS COMING TO MY SCHOOL TODAY*
- *THE WEATHERPERSON'S HANDBOOK*
- *IF NOT FOR WEATHER WE WOULD ALL BE NAKED!*
- *SKEETER'S FIRST FLIGHT*
- *SKEETER'S ISLAND ADVENTURE*

BOOK ORDERS

To inquire about purchasing this book or
any other book by Christopher Nance call:
1 -888-831-9268 (toll free)

OR WRITE

Christopher Productions, Inc.
10153 $^1/_2$ Riverside Drive #266
Toluca Lake, California   91602

VISA, MasterCard, Discover or American Express accepted.
PLEASE DO NOT SEND CASH.
Checks made payable to: **C.P.I. Publishers**
Returned checks are subject to the service charge of $15 or the
minimum allowed by state law.

BOOK SIGNINGS

Please contact us at the above phone number or address if you are
having a large book fair at your school, church or service organization
and would like Christopher Nance to attend for a book signing.

FAN CLUB & NEWSLETTER

If you would like to join the Christopher Nance fan club,
"THE WEATHER DUDE," and be on our mailing list to receive a
free and fun newsletter, send the following information to our
office address listed above: Name, Address, Age and Birthday.

VISIT US AT: WWW.WEATHERDUDE.COM